For Steve and Matthew

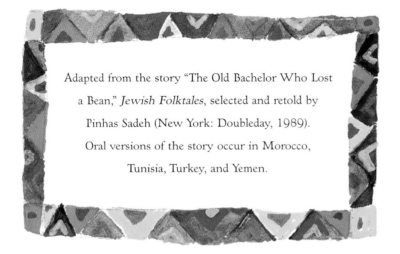

Adapted from the story "The Old Bachelor Who Lost

a Bean," *Jewish Folktales*, selected and retold by

Pinhas Sadeh (New York: Doubleday, 1989).

Oral versions of the story occur in Morocco,

Tunisia, Turkey, and Yemen.

Copyright © 2003 by Shelley Fowles
All rights reserved
First published in Great Britain by Frances Lincoln Limited, 2003
Printed and bound in Singapore
First American edition, 2003
1 3 5 7 9 10 8 6 4 2

Library of Congress Cataloging-in-Publication Data
Fowles, Shelley.
    The bachelor and the bean / Shelley Fowles.— 1st American ed.
        p.   cm.
    Summary: In this Jewish folktale from Morocco, a bachelor receives a magic pot from
an imp, but it is stolen by an old woman.
    ISBN 0-374-30478-5
    [1. Jews—Folklore.   2. Folklore—Morocco.]   I. Title.

PZ8.1.F8182 Bac 2003
398.2'089'924—dc21

2002023160

The Bachelor
and the
Bean

Shelley Fowles

Farrar, Straus and Giroux
New York

Once, long ago, there was a grumpy old bachelor who lived in a little town in Morocco.

One day he bought a snack of cooked beans in the market. But just before he could finish it, the last bean dropped into a well.

"My bean, my bean!" he yelled.

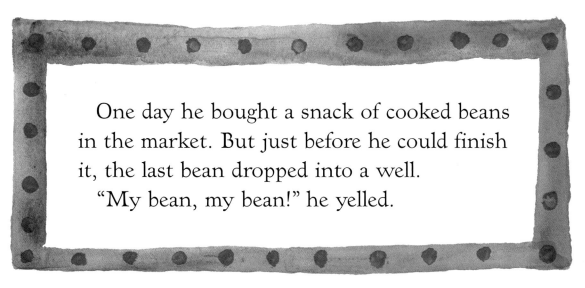

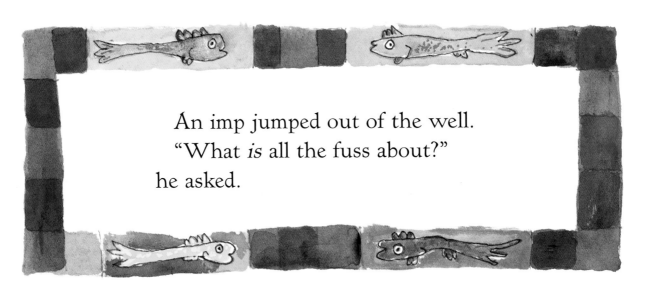

An imp jumped out of the well.
"What *is* all the fuss about?"
he asked.

"Give me back my bean!" the angry old bachelor shouted.

"By the hair of my grandmother's beard! It is only a miserable bean!" exclaimed the imp. "Look, here is a magic pot. Ask for whatever you want to eat, and it will appear. Only keep the noise down—I hate a racket!"

And with these words, the imp dove back into his well.

"Pot, give me a tasty stew with almonds and raisins," said the bachelor, feeling a bit silly.

To his amazement, he got his wish: a delicious stew appeared inside his new pot!

The bachelor showed the wonderful pot to all his neighbors, asking them to order whatever they pleased. They were thrilled, and everyone was happy. Everyone, that is, except one jealous old lady.

"I'll come back tonight and swap it for one of my own," she thought. "He'll never notice!"

So that is what she did.

But the bachelor soon discovered that the pot
stayed empty when he asked it for food.

He went back to the well.

"Hey, you! Imp!" the bachelor said rudely.
"Your pot doesn't work. It's worn out already.
Give me another one!"

The imp looked at the pot.

"This is not the pot I gave you, and I had only one
like it. I'm not made of pots! Take this other one instead.
Ask it for plates, cups, that sort of thing," he snapped,
"and leave me alone!"

He dove back into the well with a bad-tempered splash.

The new pot proved to be even better than the first one. It filled up with any vessels and plates the bachelor asked for, and they were all of solid gold, silver, and crystal. The bachelor was delighted and told all his neighbors.

But once again the jealous old lady stole his pot—
only this time she didn't bother to replace it.

The bachelor went back to the imp.

"You again!" the imp grumbled. "I heard what happened. People are talking about it all over the market. Well, I have one last pot for you. Fill it with water and look inside—and don't come back!"

The old bachelor filled the pot with water and gazed
into it.

Slowly a picture formed of the jealous old lady with
the stolen pots.

He rushed to her house and banged on the door.
"Give me back my pots, you old biddy!"
A voice shrieked back at him, "Who are you
calling an old biddy? You can't have the pots back.
They are mine now!"

The old bachelor was amazed. Such a strong voice! Such a nasty temper! Such awful manners . . . What a wonderful woman! How they would shout at each other! They were a perfect match.

"Marry me, you silly old biddy," he yelled, "and then the pots will belong to both of us!"

So the grumpy old bachelor got his pots and a wife. They had a huge wedding party with food from one pot and tableware from the other.

And from then on, I am happy to say, their quarrels could be heard from one end of town to the other!